I have this little sister Lola.
She is small and very funny.
Sometimes Lola likes to play
with my things.
Usually I don't mind.

One day I come home from school
with the best thing I have ever made.

Lola says, "Ooooh!"

I say,
"It took me **ten** days,
    three hours and **forty** minutes
to make the outside,
        which is called
the **superstructure**...

"... It's built from

 three

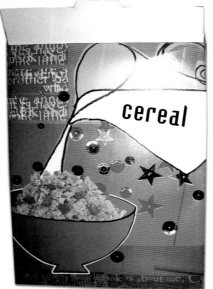 cereal

packets,

ten
yoghurt
pots,

28 bottle tops,

157

sweet

wrappers

and

a roll

of

extra-wide
tinfoil."

Lola says, "Ooooh!"

I say, "Don't touch it!
This rocket is really breakable.
I don't mind you playing with
most of my things,
but you must double,
triple promise
you'll NEVER play
with it."

"Let's play something
        else then," says Lola.
    I say, "I've promised to play football
        with Marv."
"But what am I going to do?" says Lola.
        And I say, "Why don't you play
    with Soren Lorensen?"

Soren Lorensen is Lola's imaginary friend.
No one can see him except for Lola.

And Lola says,
    "Soren Lorensen always wants
to play with me."

"Hello, Soren Lorensen," says Lola.
"Charlie's gone to play football with Marv,
so we can play a very good game,
can't we?"

And Soren Lorensen says,
    "Yes, with those two hyenas
that are brothers and twins and
that tiny small elephant."

Lola says, "Oh yes, Ellie.

"Where will the adventure be?"

Soren Lorensen says,
"The place where all the **animals** live."

And Lola says,
"In **Animal** Land."

Soren Lorensen says, "Ellie is really sad because he doesn't like the nasty hyenas laughing at him."

"Those **hyenas** are **meanies**, aren't they?" says Lola.
"What are we going to do?"

"We can't leave Ellie all **sad**," says Lola.
"He must go back to all his nice friends in **Animal** Land...
but **how** are we going to get him there?"

Then Soren Lorensen points to the rocket.

Lola says,
"But that is an extremely breakable and special rocket
and Charlie said that we should never,
NEVER touch it or play with it."

"But I think what Charlie meant was that if
we did play with it, we must be extra
specially careful," says Soren Lorensen.

So Lola reaches up to get the rocket.

Soren Lorensen says,
  "Remember to be extra
specially careful, Lola."

And Lola says,

"I am!
  I am!"

Then she says,

"Oh no!"

Lola looks at the pieces of broken rocket.
"You know, I think that when
things are broken they can always be
mended and made like new..."

"If we both act normally, Lola,
then Charlie might not think
we did it," says Soren Lorensen.

Lola whispers,
"No, he'll never know."

When I get home I shout,
"My rocket!
Lola!
Did you break
    my rocket?"

Lola says,
"I didn't break your
    rocket, Charlie."

I say,
"You are telling a big lie, Lola!
And you know it!"

"Don't tell Mum!"
says Lola. "Wait, Charlie!
    I just have to quickly talk
to Soren Lorensen."

Lola says, "Do you think we should tell him
what really happened?"
Soren Lorensen says, "Maybe we could tell Charlie
somebody else broke the rocket?"
And Lola says, "Yes! Because it is nearly true!"

So Lola comes to talk to me.
"Charlie, Soren Lorensen and me have got something
very **extremely** important to tell you."

I say, "What?"

Lola says,
"It is the real **true** story of who **broke**
your special **rocket**.

"Well, me and Soren Lorensen were
playing in our room, Charlie,
and Ellie needed to go
in your rocket.

I didn't think it
was a good idea,
but he had to get away.

So we **squeezed**
Ellie, and it was
a real **squish**.
But we **did** it.

And then we **took off**.

Whoosh! Whoosh!

"... and then
we landed

and
we
were
so
squished
that...

the
rocket
just fell
to
P i e c e s.
And that's
what happened."

I say,
"Right.
I'm going to
tell **Mum!**"

"Oh dear, I don't think he **believed** us," says Soren Lorensen.

Lola says,
"I think I have to tell
Charlie the **truth**. But will it
make Charlie **like** me again?"

Soren Lorensen says,
"As long as you say **sorry** too."

Lola knocks at the door.
"Soren Lorensen
really wants to say sorry
for breaking your
rocket, Charlie."

So I just shut
the door.

Then there's another knock
and Lola says,
"It was me that broke
your rocket. Just as I was
getting your extremely
special rocket down from
the really high shelf...
it fell and broke
into lots
of pieces.

I am really ever so sorry
for breaking your
extremely special rocket,
Charlie."

And I say,
"Are you **really**, Lola?"

Lola says, "**Sorry**, Charlie."

And she does look really very sorry.

So I say, "That's OK.
At least you've told the truth."

Then Lola sees the rocket.

"You **mended** it, Charlie!" she says.

And I say,
"Yes, Lola, I've **mended** it."

"I like it," says Lola.
I say,
"Don't touch it!"